Mexican Heritage

Celebrating Diversity in My Classroom

By Tamra B. Orr

21st Century **Junior** Library

Published in the United States of America by
Cherry Lake Publishing
Ann Arbor, Michigan
www.cherrylakepublishing.com

Reading Adviser: Marla Conn MS, Ed., Literacy specialist, Read-Ability, Inc.

Photo Credits: © Bill Perry / Shutterstock Images, cover; © ThiagoSantos / Shutterstock Images, 4; © Marcelo Rodriguez / Shutterstock Images, 6; © VICTOR TORRES / Shutterstock Images, 8; © Elena Elisseeva / Shutterstock Images, 10; © Byelikova Oksana / Shutterstock Images, 12; © BestStockFoto / Shutterstock Images, 14; © VVDVVD / Shutterstock Images, 16; © miker / Shutterstock Images, 18; © Kobby Dagan / Shutterstock Images, 20

Library of Congress Cataloging-in-Publication Data
Name: Orr, Tamra B., author.
Title: Mexican heritage / by Tamra B. Orr.
Description: Ann Arbor : Cherry Lake Publishing, [2018] | Series: Celebrating diversity in my classroom | Includes bibliographical references and index. | Audience: Grades K-3.
Identifiers: LCCN 2017035389 | ISBN 9781534107335 (hardcover) | ISBN 9781534109315 (pdf) | ISBN 9781534108325 (pbk.) | ISBN 9781534120303 (hosted ebook)
Subjects: LCSH: Mexico—Social life and customs—Juvenile literature. | Mexico—Civilization—Juvenile literature.
Classification: LCC F1208.5 .O78 2018 | DDC 972—dc23
LC record available at https://lccn.loc.gov/2017035389

Cherry Lake Publishing would like to acknowledge the work of The Partnership for 21st Century Skills.
Please visit *www.p21.org* for more information.

Printed in the United States of America
Corporate Graphics

CONTENTS

5 **Marvelous Mexico**

7 **Hola Amigo!**

11 **The Sound of Church Bells**

15 **Flavor and Spice**

19 **Battles and Mariachi Bands**

22 Glossary

23 Find Out More

24 Index

24 About the Author

Mexico is popular with tourists because of its famous beaches and charming towns.

Marvelous Mexico

Mexico is the 14th-largest country in the world. It is part of North America. More than 120 million people call the country home. People from Mexico have also **emigrated** to other countries all over the world. There are about 11.7 million **immigrants** from Mexico in the United States!

What is their home country like? Read ahead to find out!

Traditional artwork and crafts are sold in many town squares.

Hola Amigo!

"*Hola amigo!*" That means "Hello, friend!" in Spanish. Mexico's main language is Spanish. Someone from Mexico may ask you, "*Como te llamas?*" It means, "What is your name?"

The Spanish language is different from English. For example, the letter *h* is silent. That is why *hola* is said "o-la." The letter *j* is pronounced like an English *h*. The spicy

Charreada is a competition similar to rodeo that came to Mexico from Spain in the 1500s.

pepper *jalapeño* is "ha-la-pen-yo." When two *l*'s are put together, it makes a *y* sound. So *llama* becomes "ya-ma."

More than 50 million people in the United States know how to speak Spanish. It is the second most common language in the country, next to English. That is a lot of amigos!

Ask Questions!

Do you know how to speak Spanish? Do any of your friends or teachers? What words or sentences would you like to learn the most?

There are Catholic churches in cities and towns all over Mexico.

The Sound of Church Bells

You are probably used to hearing bells ring every day in school. The people in Mexico are also used to hearing the sound of bells. Church bells. Catholic church bells ring out loudly every day in many towns and cities. They ring to welcome in a new morning and again at noon. They ring at night, as the sun sets. Bells ring to let

The Feast of Our Lady of Guadalupe is a popular festival for many Catholics in Mexico.

everyone know that two people just got married. They also ring to say a life has been lost.

Most of the people from Mexico are Catholic. They believe in **miracles** and **saints**. One of their favorite saints is Our Lady of Guadalupe. She appeared hundreds of years ago. She asked a man to build a church on the spot where she stood. Then she disappeared. It was a miracle! A church was built right away. Today, drawings and statues of Our Lady are found almost everywhere throughout Mexico.

Tamales are pockets of dough filled with meats and spices,
then wrapped in corn husks and steamed.

Flavor and Spice

From spicy peppers to refried beans. From sizzling fajitas to crunchy tacos. Mexico is a land of delicious food. Many of the country's dishes have traveled to the United States. Have you ever tried one?

Many Americans grab two pieces of bread. They add a few of their favorite ingredients and make a sandwich. In Mexico, people grab flour or corn *tortillas*. Next, they add

Food can also be sweet! Sugar and cinnamon *churros* are a great treat.

rice, beans, meat, **salsa**, sour cream, or *guacamole*. Then they roll up the tortilla. It's time to eat! Tortillas are used to make burritos, enchiladas, quesadillas, and tacos.

Mexican food can be very spicy. That's because of peppers like jalapeños or *chiles*.

Some confuse Cinco de Mayo with Mexico's Independence Day, but these are two different celebrations honoring different events.

Battles and Mariachi Bands

More than 150 years ago, Mexican and French soldiers went to battle. They were fighting for control of Mexico. The battle was fought in the town of Puebla on May 5. The people of Mexico won, and ever since then, Cinco de Mayo has been celebrated in Puebla. The holiday is also celebrated throughout the United States, especially in large cities in California and Texas.

San Diego, California's Cinco de Mayo celebration is the largest of its kind in America.

If you go to a Cinco de Mayo celebration in your city, listen carefully. Do you hear exciting music? That is a *mariachi* band. These bands are found at many events celebrating Mexico's history and people.

Some mariachi bands have a few people. Others have a dozen. Mariachi bands usually have violins, trumpets, and guitars. Every player sings!

Look!

Look at this photo of dancers at a Cinco de Mayo celebration. Do you think they are having fun? What would it be like to dance and dress up in costumes like these?

GLOSSARY

emigrated (EM-ih-grayt-id) left your home country to live in another country

immigrants (IM-ih-gruhnts) people who have moved from one country to another and settled there

miracles (MIR-uh-kuhlz) extraordinary events that are thought to come from God

saints (SAYNTS) people of great holiness

salsa (SAHL-suh) a hot sauce made with various peppers, onions, and tomatoes

Spanish Words

amigo (ah-MEE-go) friend

chiles (CHEE-lays) a type of spicy pepper

churros (CHUR-ohs) a Mexican dessert made with sugar, flour, and cinnamon

Como te llamas? (KOH-moh TEH YAH-mas) What is your name?

guacamole (gwa-kah-mole-ee) a dip made with avocados

hola (OH-la) hello

jalapeño (ha-la-PEN-yo) a spicy pepper

mariachi (mar-ee-AH-chee) type of band or Mexican music

tortillas (tor-TEE-yas) wraps for food, usually made with corn flour

FIND OUT MORE

BOOKS

Moon, Walt. *Let's Explore Mexico.* Minneapolis: Lerner Publications, 2017.

Perkins, Chloe. *Mexico.* New York: Simon Spotlight, 2016.

Tieck, Sarah. *Mexico.* Minneapolis: ABDO Publishing, 2014.

WEBSITES

Ducksters—Mexico
www.ducksters.com/geography/country/mexico.php
Learn more facts about the geography, people, economy, and government of Mexico.

Mexico Facts
www.kids-world-travel-guide.com/mexico-facts.html
Read interesting facts about Mexico.

National Geographic Kids—Mexico
http://kids.nationalgeographic.com/explore/countries/
mexico/#mexico-dancers.jpg
Find out more about Mexico, including its history, people, geography, and culture.

INDEX

A
arts and crafts, 6

B
bells, 11, 13

C
Catholics, 10, 11,
    12, 13
charreada, 8
churros, 16
Cinco de Mayo, 18–21

F
festivals, 12
food, 14, 15–17

H
holidays, 18–21

I
immigrants, 5

L
language, 7, 9

M
mariachi bands, 21
Mexico
    population, 5
    size, 5
miracles, 13
music, 21

R
religion, 10–13

S
Spanish, 7, 9

T
tamales, 14
tortillas, 15, 17
tourists, 4

ABOUT THE AUTHOR

Tamra Orr is the author of hundreds of books for readers of all ages. She graduated from Ball State University, but moved with her husband and four children to Oregon in 2001. She is a full-time author, and when she isn't researching and writing, she writes letters to friends all over the world. Orr enjoys life in the big city of Portland and feels very lucky to be surrounded by so much diversity.